T0120338

Men-of-War

The Works of Patrick O'Brian

The Aubrey/Maturin Novels in order of publication
MASTER AND COMMANDER
POST CAPTAIN
HMS SURPRISE
THE MAURITIUS COMMAND
DESOLATION ISLAND
THE FORTUNE OF WAR
THE SURGEON'S MATE
THE IONIAN MISSION
TREASON'S HARBOUR
THE FAR SIDE OF THE WORLD
THE REVERSE OF THE MEDAL
THE LETTER OF MARQUE
THE THIRTEEN-GUN SALUTE
THE NUTMEG OF CONSOLATION
CLARISSA OAKES
THE WINE-DARK SEA
THE COMMODORE
THE YELLOW ADMIRAL
THE HUNDRED DAYS
BLUE AT THE MIZZEN
THE FINAL UNFINISHED VOYAGE OF JACK AUBREY

Nautical Novels
THE GOLDEN OCEAN
THE UNKNOWN SHORE

Other Novels
CAESAR
HUSSEIN
TESTIMONIES
THE CATALANS
THE ROAD TO SAMARCAND
RICHARD TEMPLE

Short Fiction
BEASTS ROYAL
THE COMPLETE SHORT STORIES

Non-fiction
MEN-OF-WAR: LIFE IN NELSON'S NAVY
PICASSO
JOSEPH BANKS

Anthology
A BOOK OF VOYAGES

Poetry
THE UNCERTAIN LAND AND OTHER POEMS

Men-of-War

PATRICK O'BRIAN

HarperCollins*Publishers*

HarperCollins*Publishers*
1 London Bridge Street
London SE1 9GF

HarperCollinsPublishers
Macken House, 39/40 Mayor Street Upper
Dublin 1, D01 C9W8, Ireland

www.harpercollins.co.uk

This edition 2023

2

First published in Great Britain by Collins 1974

Copyright © The Estate of the late Patrick O'Brian CBE 1974

'Jack Aubrey's Ships' © Brian Lavery 1994

Patrick O'Brian asserts the moral right
to be identified as the author of this work

ISBN 978-0-00-835599-9

Printed and bound in the UK using
100% Renewable Electricity at CPI Group (UK) Ltd

All rights reserved. No part of this publication may be
reproduced, stored in a retrieval system, or transmitted, in any form
or by any means, electronic, mechanical, photocopying, recording or
otherwise, without the prior written permission of the publishers.

This book is produced from independently certified FSC™ paper
to ensure responsible forest management.

For more information visit: www.harpercollins.co.uk/green

CONTENTS

Introduction   1

The Ships   5

The Guns   19

The Ship's Company   31

Life at Sea   51

Songs   69

'Jack Aubrey's Ships'
by Brian Lavery   77

Men-of-War

Introduction

Since Britain is an island, it has always needed a navy to keep enemies from coming over the sea to invade it. If there had been an efficient navy in Roman times neither Caesar nor Claudius could have crossed the Channel; if there had been one in 1066, William would never have been called the Conqueror; and if there had *not* been one in the Armada year the British might be speaking Spanish now. Without the Royal Navy to stop him, Napoleon would certainly have invaded England in 1805 (he had 2,293 vessels in the Channel ports ready to carry 161,215 men and 9,059 horses across), just as Hitler would have done in 1940.

Then again, since England has been a trading nation time out of mind, it has always needed a navy to protect its merchant ships and to attack the enemy's sea-borne trade. And ever since England became an industrial country as well, unable to produce enough food for its greatly increased population, a navy has been essential to prevent its being starved into surrender.

A navy has always been necessary; but it was not for many centuries after King Alfred's time that the Royal Navy as we know it, a permanent service quite separate from the mercantile marine, came into being. The kings generally had some ships of their own, but in war most of the country's naval force was made up of merchantmen, some hired and some provided by such towns as the Cinque Ports; and once the war was over they went home: they were not real men-of-war, in the sense of being ships specially built and armed for fighting alone. 'Man' is an odd word for a ship, since sailors call all vessels 'she', but 'man-of-war' came into the language about 1450, and it has stayed, together with East-Indiaman for a ship going to India or Guineaman for one sailing to West Africa, and many more. Henry VIII had about fifty men-of-war, and it was he who set up the Admiralty and Navy Board to look after them. Queen Elizabeth I had fewer – of the 197 English ships that sailed to fight the Spanish Armada only 34 belonged to her. Charles I had 42, but in the wars of the Commonwealth the number grew, so that when King Charles II came into his own again he had 154 vessels of all kinds. It was at this time that the Navy began to take on its modern shape: formerly the King had had to keep his ships out of his own pocket, but now the nation paid for them; and now the officers, instead of being sent away when there was no need for them, were kept on half-pay – they could make a career of the Navy rather than join from time to time. This did not apply to the men, however: they came aboard, or were brought aboard by the press-gang, every time there was a war; and when it was over they went back to their former ways of making a living. By the end of Charles II's reign the Royal Navy had 173 vessels, and because of the labours of Samuel Pepys, the Secretary of the Admiralty, and of the Duke of York, who was Lord High Admiral, it was a fairly efficient body.

All through the eighteenth century the Royal Navy grew: in 1714 there were 247 ships amounting to 167,219 tons; in 1760 412 of 321,104 tons; and in 1793, although the number had dropped by one, the tonnage amounted to 402,555. This was at the beginning of the great war with France, in which the Royal Navy reached the height of its glory, and the numbers increased rapidly; by the time Napoleon had been dealt with, Britain had no less than 776 vessels, counting all she had taken from the French, Spaniards, Danes and Dutch; and altogether they came to 724,810 tons. At this time, at its greatest expansion, the Royal Navy needed 113,000 seamen and 31,400 Royal Marines, and a hard task it was to find them, as we shall see when we come to the press-gang.

The Ships

The vessels that made up the early Navy were of all shapes and sizes, from Henry VIII's *Henry Grace à Dieu* of 1,000 tons down to row-barges, passing by cogs, carracks, and ballingers, shallops and pinnaces; but by the seventeenth century the pattern that lasted up until the coming of steam was clear, and by the eighteenth it was firmly established. The ships of the Royal Navy were divided into six rates as early as Charles I, and this is how they stood in 1793:

FIRST RATE 100–112 guns, 841 men (including officers, seamen, boys and servants)

SECOND RATE 90–98 guns, 743 men

THIRD RATE 64, 74 and 80 guns, 494, about 620, and 724 men

FOURTH RATE 50 guns, 345 men (this rate also included 60-gun ships, but there was none in 1793)

| FIFTH RATE | 32, 36, 38 and 44 guns, 217–297 men |
| SIXTH RATE | 20, 24 and 28 guns, 138, 158 and 198 men. |

All these ships, from 20 to 112 guns, were commanded by post-captains.

Vessels that carried less than 20 guns – that is to say, all the sloops, brigs, bomb-ketches, fire-ships, cutters and so on – were not rated, and their captains were masters and commanders in the case of sloops, and lieutenants in the rest. ('Captains' in the sense of commanding officers, not of permanent rank: if a midshipman was sent away in charge of a prize, he was her captain so long as he was in command.)

The ships that carried 60 guns and more were called ships of the line, because it was they alone that could stand in the line of battle when two fleets came into action. The first and second rates were three-deckers (that is to say they had three whole decks of guns, apart from those on the quarterdeck and forecastle); the third and fourth rates and the 44s were two-deckers; and the rest one-deckers – they were frigates from 38 guns down to 26, and post-ships when they carried 24 or 20. The word 'frigate' was used in the seventeenth century without any very precise meaning, but by this time it had long been understood to mean a ship that carried her main armament on one deck and that was built for speed: the frigates were the eyes of the fleet, and they were also excellent cruisers, capital for independent action.

In 1793, counting those that were being built or repaired, those that were laid up and those that were stationary harbour ships, the Royal Navy had 153 ships of the line, 43 50- and 44-gun two-deckers, 99 frigates, and 102 unrated vessels.

I say vessels rather than ships because, although a vessel means anything that floats or is meant to float, for a sailor a ship is something quite distinct: it is a vessel, of course, but it is a square-rigged vessel with three masts (fore, main and mizen) and a bowsprit; what is more these three masts must be made up of a lower-mast, topmast and topgallant-mast, and anything with only two masts (such as a brig) or with three all in one piece (such as a polacre) that presumed to call itself a ship would have been laughed to scorn, hooted down, given no countenance whatsoever.

The most usual line-of-battle ship was the 74: there were 73 of them at the beginning of the war and 137 in 1816. A 74 weighed about 1,700 tons and she needed some 2,000 oak trees to build her – 57 acres of forest. In the 1790s England could supply much of the wood, but as the years went by the forests began to look very thin, for an oak tree does not spring up overnight; and at least half the timber had to be imported. It was always oak, the very best oak, for nothing else would bear the terrible strain of the winter storms or the shock of battle: fir was tried for frigates and cedar for smaller craft, but it did not answer – heart of oak was the only thing for a man-of-war. Masts and yards had to be imported too: they were made of fir, and they had to be very long and straight. The mainmast of a first-rate was made up of three sections 117, 70 and 35 feet long, while her main yard was 102 feet across – such trees could be found in large numbers only in America or the north.

The building of a man-of-war was a highly-skilled, long and complicated business that I could not describe in less than ten volumes, but roughly this is how they set about it. First the ship was worked out on paper, sometimes following the plans of the beautiful and fast-sailing French or Spanish ships that were captured; then a model might be made, usually to the scale of a quarter of an inch to the foot (there are a great many of these models in the Maritime Museum at Greenwich and several in the London Science Museum); and then the keel would be laid, generally in one of the royal dockyards but sometimes in private shipbuilders' yards. The keel was a massive assembly of elm, and to this were fixed the great rib-like oak timbers, first the stem (in front) and then the stern-post to take the rudder; then came the midship floor-timber and all the rest of the ship's framework. When this was done the ribs were planked inside and out and the beams laid across. The decks were laid on the beams, with proper places for the masts, and when the hull was finished it was divided up by bulkheads into store-rooms, powder-magazines, cabins and so on, with ladders for going up and down, and the whole of the hull that was to be under water was coppered against the attacks of the teredo, a sea-worm that used to pierce holes right through the bottom, before this plating was thought of halfway through the eighteenth century.

All this took a long time – the *Victory*, for example, was laid down in 1759 but not launched until 1765 – and seeing that the wood was out in all weathers it often began to rot even before the ship was finished. The truth of the matter is that most of the British ships were not nearly so well built as the French or Spanish: they were often slow; they nearly always carried too many guns; they were sometimes very crank – that is, they leaned over in a wind so that they could not open the lower gun-port or the sea would rush in; and occasionally they fell to pieces in a storm. Among the worst were the Forty Thieves, forty ships of the line that were all built in private yards by dishonest contractors, and that were looked upon as floating coffins: but sometimes the royal yards were not much better. Nevertheless, the Royal Navy won all the great fleet battles and nearly all the smaller actions between ships of roughly equal force. They did so partly out of force of habit, partly by better gunnery, and even more by better seamanship – you can only learn to be a sailor at sea, and the English Navy was at sea all the year

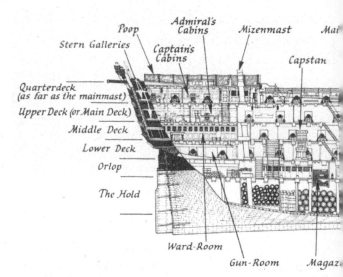

A first-rate ship, the *Victory*, in cross-section.

round, whatever the weather, whereas the French and Spaniards were shut up in their harbours.

Now I will say something about the decks, and the sails and rigging, although the pictures show these things better than any number of words. Suppose we were transported to the bottom of a three-decker: we should be in the hold, a vast dark space about 150 feet long, 50 wide and 20 high, with curving sides, with a good many rats in it and a horrible smell of bilge-water – no fresh air and no light, because it

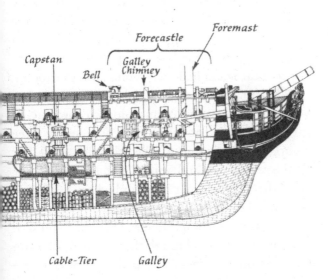

would be well under the water-line. Most of it would be taken up with ballast, fresh water in casks, casks of salt pork and beef – enough to feed eight hundred men for six months – the cloth-lined powder magazine, the tin-lined bread-room, and all sorts of other stores. Overhead would be the orlop-deck, near the water-line. Right aft on the orlop was the cockpit, where the older midshipmen lived and where the wounded were treated in battle; forward of the cockpit were cabins for the junior officers – little dark, airless cupboards; then the sail-room with the spare sails; then the cable-tiers, where the great cables were stowed (some were 25 inches round, and all were 101 fathoms long); then the fore-cockpit where the boatswain and carpenter had their cabins and store rooms. Above the orlop was the lower deck, where the first and heaviest tier of guns stood in two rows facing their gun-ports, 32-pounders, weighing nearly three tons apiece. This was also called the mess-deck, for here the seamen ate and slept. Right aft lay the gunroom, where the gunner lived and where the junior midshipmen slung their hammocks; and right forward was the manger, a compartment designed to prevent the water that came through the hawse-holes from sweeping along the deck – it was also the place where the ship's pigs, sheep and cattle were kept. Above the lower deck came the middle deck, with its rows of 24-pounders; and above that the upper or main deck, with its 18-pounders. The ward-room, where the senior officers messed, was at the after end, and their cabins usually opened off it. Still higher, from the stern to the mainmast, ran the quarterdeck, and on the same level as the quarterdeck, from the fore-shrouds to the bows, the forecastle, the one with ten 12-pounders and the other with two: the quarterdeck and forecastle were connected by gangways. Lastly, above the after part of the quarterdeck, from the mizenmast to the stern, there was the poop, the roof of the captain's quarters – his sleeping cabin, his fore-cabin, and his beautiful great after-cabin which opened on to a stern-gallery (very like a balcony) where he could walk and admire the view in privacy.

But here we are speaking of a first-rate, a three-decker, and many three-deckers were flagships – that is, they had an admiral aboard. When this was so, the great man occupied the after end of the main deck, just under the captain, and the lieutenants and their ward-room moved down to the middle deck.

In the case of two-deckers, the arrangement was much the same, only the middle deck was left out; but in one-deckers, such as frigates, there was no poop – the captain's cabin was under the quarterdeck, on the main deck, and the lieutenants took over the gun-room on the deck below for their mess, banishing the gunner to a cabin forward and the younger midshipmen to the cockpit.

Now for the sails and the rigging. A square-rigged ship had three masts, of course, and these masts were held up by shrouds on each side, by stays to keep them from pitching backwards, and by back-stays to keep them from pitching forward: the shrouds had ratlines

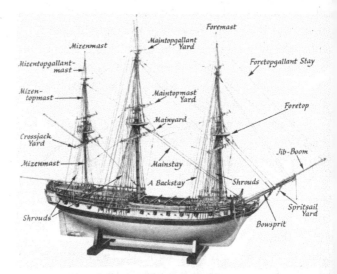

Masts, yards and rigging on a 28-gun frigate.

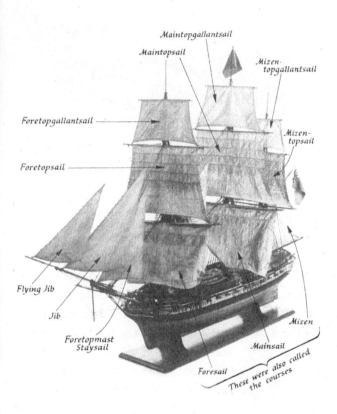

Maintopgallantsail

Maintopsail

Mizen topgallantsail

Foretopgallantsail

Mizen-topsail

Foretopsail

Flying Jib

Jib

Foretopmast Staysail

Mizen

Mainsail

Foresail

These were also called the courses

Sails on a frigate.

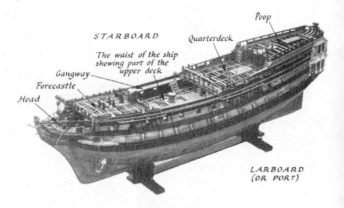

A two-decker with her bowsprit and masts out and her deck-planking removed to show the construction.

across them, to make ladders up which the seamen could climb to reach the upper rigging and the sails; and the first set of shrouds led to the platform called the top, or fighting-top, which stood at the junction of the lower-mast and topmast and which served to spread the shrouds for the next section of mast – these masts, by the way, were made to slide up and down through the top, so that in an emergency the top-gallantmasts and even topmasts could be struck down on deck. The masts had yards slung across them horizontally, and it was to these yards that the most important sails were attached. The mainmast had a mainyard for the mainsail, a maintopmast yard for its topsail, a maintopgallant yard, and above that, in fine weather, a royal yard: the foremast had the same four yards with fore tacked on to their names: the lowest yard on the mizen, however, was called the crossjack, which hardly ever had a sail spread on it, because the chief sail on the mizen was a fore-and-aft sail spread by a gaff or lateen over the poop; the rest of its yards were the same. The bowsprit too had its yards and sails – the spritsail and the spritsail-topsail. There were other sails spread on the stays and various booms, but these were the important ones.

When the wind was from behind and the sails were spread, obviously the ship was pushed forward – not that this was the best point of sailing, because if the breeze were right astern, the after sails would becalm the rest, whereas if it came from her quarter, or 45° abaft the beam, it would fill them all. But when the wind came from the beam, that is to say sideways, or at right-angles to the ship's length, then the square sails would have been useless unless they could swing round to catch its force. And of course that is what happened: the yards were pulled round with braces and the lower corners of the sails were hauled round too – the sheet on the lower leeward corner was hauled aft and the tack, the rope on the windward lower corner, was hauled forward, so that the sail continued to draw; and seeing that the ship could not be forced sideways through the water it went on going forward, though a little sideways too – this sideways motion was called its leeway. Indeed, even when the wind was more from in front than sideways, the ship could still go on: a square-rigged ship, close-hauled, that is, with her yards braced up sharp to an angle of 20° with the keel, could sail within six points of the wind, or 63° 45' from it – or in other words, if the wind were coming from the north, she could still sail east-north-east.

So much for the ships: now for the guns.

The Guns

The early guns had beautiful names like cannon-royal, cannon-serpentine, demi-culverin and falconet, but they had a bewildering variety of shot and charge; and since these weapons, together with basilisks, sakers and murdering-pieces might all be mounted on the same deck, it led to sad confusion in time of battle.

By the eighteenth century there were many fewer kinds, and they were called by the weight of the shot they fired: a first-rate, for example, carried 30 32-pounders on her lower deck, 28 24-pounders on her middle deck, 30 18-pounders on her upper deck, 10 12-pounders on her quarterdeck and 2 on her forecastle, thus firing a broadside of 1,158 lb. Everything was plain and straightforward: each deck had guns, shot, cartridges and wads of the same size; the guns could be supplied from the magazines as fast as the powder-boys could run; and all that remained was to fire them as quickly and accurately as possible.

This was something of a task, however, for the gun was a massive brute, mounted on a wheeled carriage, and it had to be fired from a deck that might be in violent motion. An 18-pounder, a medium-sized gun, had a barrel nine feet long; it weighed 2,388 lb, and it needed a crew of ten to handle it, for not only did it have to be run in and out, but it had to be kept under rigid control – two tons of metal careering about the deck in a rough sea could kill people and smash through the ship's side.

The crew included the captain of the gun, the second captain, a sponger, a fireman, some boarders and sail-trimmers, and a powder-boy, with perhaps a couple of Marines to help in the heaving. They were used to working together, and in crack ships they handled their monsters with wonderful skill: it was English gunnery rather than English ships that won the great naval battles. Each man had his own particular job, so in the roar of battle there was no need for orders. When a gun was to be fired the port was opened, the tight lashings that held the gun to the side were cast loose, and the tompion (the bung that kept the muzzle water-tight) taken out. The men hooked on the tackles – one to each side to heave the gun up to the port and the train-tackle behind to run it inboard for loading – and they seized the breeching to the knob at the end of the gun. This breeching was a stout rope made fast to ring-bolts in the ship's side, and it was long enough to let the gun recoil.

Now, with the gun run in and held by the breeching and the train-tackle, the sponger took the cartridge, a flannel bag with six pounds of powder in it, from the powder-boy, rammed it down the muzzle until the captain felt it in the breech with the priming-iron that he thrust through the touch-hole and cried 'Home!' Then the 18-pound shot went down, followed by a wad, both rammed hard: the men clapped on to the side-tackles and ran the loaded gun up, its muzzle as far out as it would go. The captain stabbed the cartridge with his iron, filled the hole and the pan above it with powder from his horn, and the gun was ready to fire, either by a spark from a flint-lock or by a slow-match, a kind of glowing wick. It was aimed right or left by the crew heaving the carriage with their crow-bars and handspikes; and the captain, who aimed the gun, could raise or lower it with a wedge under the breech. But although they could send a ball for well over a mile, these guns were not accurate at a distance and they were usually fired at point-blank range – about four hundred yards – or less: indeed, commanders like Nelson preferred to lay their ships yardarm to yardarm, where there was no possibility of missing, and

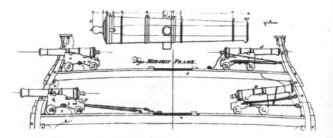

Guns on a man-of-war. The top gun on the right is run in
so that it can be loaded; both of those on the left are in the
firing position; and the lower one shows the train-tackle.
The fourth gun is housed, that is to say made fast so that
it cannot move in a heavy sea.

where their double or treble-shotted guns could fire
right through both sides of the enemy.

At the word 'Fire!' the captain stubbed the red end
of the match into the powder on the pan, the flash
ran through the touch-hole to the cartridge and the
whole thing went off with an almighty bang. The shot
flew out at 1,200 feet a second, the entire gun leapt
backwards with terrible force until it was brought up
by the breeching, and the air was filled with dense,
acrid smoke. The moment it was inboard the captain
stopped the vent, the men at the train-tackle held the
gun tight, the sponger thrust his wet mop down to

clean the barrel and put out any smouldering sparks, another cartridge, shot and wad were rammed home, and the gun was run up again, hard against the port.

It was heavy, dangerous work, above all in action, with the whole broadside firing: the low space 'tween decks would be filled with smoke; little could be seen, little heard, and the slightest false move meant the loss of a leg or an arm from the recoiling gun, to say nothing of the risks of explosion or the enemy's fire. Yet a well-trained crew could carry out the whole operation in one minute forty seconds – three broadsides in just five minutes.

They could do this even in the heat of battle, although some members of the gun-crew had other duties as well. The boarders had their cutlasses ready in their belts and they would leave the gun to batter the enemy by hand at the cry of 'Boarders away!' The sail-trimmers would go to their stations when called upon; the fireman had to be ready with his bucket to dash out the first beginnings of a flame aboard; and the second captain to see that the corresponding gun on the other side of the deck was prepared, for few ships had enough people to man two sides at once, and the same crew fought both port and starboard guns.

What they fired was mostly single round shot – the ordinary cannon-ball – and a 32-pounder could smash through two feet of solid oak at half a mile; but at close range they also used grape (a great many small balls in a canvas bag that burst when it was fired, scattering the balls over the enemy's deck and discouraging his crew), canister (much the same), and bar or chain shot to cut up his rigging.

Right through the eighteenth century the Navy used these guns with little change: the 42-pounders were laid aside as being too heavy for even a first-rate (the *Britannia*, or Old Ironsides as she was called from her massive timbers, was the last to keep them), and the 32, 24, 18, 12, 9, 6, 4 and 3-pounders were the usual armament. Then in 1779 the carronade or smasher was invented: this was a much lighter, shorter gun mounted on slides and designed for close-range fighting. It threw an enormous ball for its weight.

The first ship to be entirely armed with them, by way of experiment, was the *Rainbow*, an old 44. Before this she had carried 20 ordinary 18-pounder long guns on her lower deck, 22 12-pounders on her main deck, and two 6-pounders on her forecastle – a broad-side weight of metal of 318 lb, needing about 100 lb of powder to fire it. Now she had 20 68-pounder carronades on her lower-deck, 22 42-pounders on her main-deck, four 32-pounders on her quarterdeck and two on her forecastle – a broadside of 1,238 lb, still needing

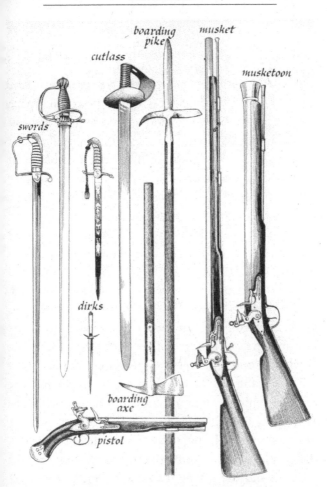

From the man-of-war's armoury, a selection of weapons.

only about 100 lb of powder, since the charge of the carronade was one twelfth of the weight of its ball, as opposed to the long gun's one third.

The *Rainbow* put to sea, and after six months she found an enemy of the right size – the powerful French 40-gun frigate *Hébé*. The action began in fine style, but to the *Rainbow*'s intense irritation it stopped almost at once. The French captain, seeing these horrible great 32-pound balls coming from the Englishman's forecastle, rightly assumed that there was even worse in store, and struck his colours.

By now it was 1782; the war was almost over and it was too late to try out the carronade in earnest. But by 1793, when the next war began, the Navy was well stocked with them, and they did splendid service in the years to come. They did not replace the long guns, however, most of the carronades being 18- or 12-pounders on the forecastle, quarterdeck and poop. Curiously enough, they were never counted in with the rest of the ship's armament, a 24-gun ship like the *Hyaena*, which mounted ten 12-pounder carronades as well as her long guns, remaining a 24-gun ship for official purposes. Firing point-blank meant firing with the gun level: to make the ball go farther one would raise the muzzle, giving it so many degrees of elevation. But point-blank was the most accurate way of firing. When a ball hit the water it would often go skipping over the surface in great bounds: the first impact, however, was by far the most deadly.

The great guns were the man-of-war's chief armament, of course; but they were not the only weapon aboard, by any means. She also carried muskets, for the use of the Marines and the small-arms men in the fighting-tops, pistols, axes and cutlasses for boarding, stinkballs (made of pitch, resin, brimstone, gunpowder and asafoetida in an earthenware pot: it was set on fire and thrown so as to burst among the enemy and overwhelm him with the stench), and grenades for tossing on to the enemy's deck, and boarding-pikes to repel him if he tried to come over the side. We might even add soot to the list, since Lord Cochrane, setting about the 32-gun frigate *El Gamo* with his 14-gun brig *Speedy* in 1803, made his men black their faces in the galley before boarding, to the unspeakable dismay of the Spaniards, who yielded less to the *Speedy*'s little 4-pounders than to the truly hideous appearance of her crew.

TABLE SHOWING THE SIZE AND WEIGHT OF LONG GUNS AND CARRONADES

	long guns	
33-pounder	9 feet 6 inches	55 cwt 21 lb
24-pounder	9 feet 6 inches	50 cwt 21 lb
18-pounder	9 feet	42 cwt 21 lb
12-pounder	9 feet	34 cwt 31 lb
12-pounder short	7 feet	21 cwt
	carronades	
68-pounder	5 feet 2 inches	36 cwt
32-pounder	4 feet ½ inch	17 cwt 14 lb
24-pounder	3 feet 11 cwt	2 qr 25 lb
18-pounder	2 feet 4 inches	8 cwt 1 qr 25 lb
12-pounder	2 feet 2 inches	5 cwt 3 qr 2 lb

TABLE SHOWING THE RANGE OF GUNS AND CARRONADES

	32-pounder carronade	*24-pounder*
point-blank	330 yards	300
5° elevation	1087 yards	1050

(the charge being one twelfth of the weight of the ball in all cases)

32, 34 and 18-pounder long guns

elevation	proportion of powder	to first graze (that is to say, where the ball first touched the water)	
2°	¼	single shot	1200 yards
2°	¼	single shot	1000 yards
2°	¼	two shot	500 yards
4°	¼	single shot	1600 yards
7°	¼	single shot	2150 yards
7°	¼	single shot	2020 yards
4°	¼	grape	1000 yards

The Ship's Company

N ow for the men who sailed the ships and fought the guns, and first the officers. Let us take a boy who wants to go to sea and follow him through his career as an officer from bottom to top; and let him be a courageous boy with a cast-iron digestion and lucky enough not to put his head in the way of a cannon-ball, so that he may stay the course. He is a typical boy of quite good family – probably a sea-officer's son or, like Nelson and Jane Austen's brothers, a parson's – but he is not highly educated, since he goes to sea when he is twelve or fourteen, and he has not had much time for school. (Officially the earliest age was eleven for officers' sons and thirteen for the rest, but no one took much notice of the regulation – seven-year-olds were not unknown.) Before he can go to sea his people have to find some captain who is willing to take him aboard, for this is almost the only way to become an officer. They succeed, and the young hero joins his ship with his sea-chest: it is filled to over-flowing, since the captain has not only insisted on the boy's parents giving him an allowance of as much as £50 a year if it is anything like a crack ship, but he will also have sent them a list of necessities. Here is a moderate example:

  1 uniform coat superfine cloth
  1 uniform coat second best
  1 round jacket suit
  1 surtout coat and watch-coat
  3 pairs of white jean trowsers and waistcoats
  3 pairs of nankeen ditto and 3 kerseymere waistcoats
  2 round hats with gold loop and cockade
  1 glazed hat, hanger (or dirk) and belt
 18 linen shirts, frilled
 12 plain calico shirts
  3 black silk handkerchiefs
 12 pocket cotton ditto
 12 pairs of brown cotton stockings
  6 pairs of white cotton stockings
  6 pairs worsted or lamb's wool stockings
  2 strong pairs of shoes and 2 light pairs
  6 towels and 3 pairs of sheets and pillow-cases
  2 table-cloths about 3 yards long

A mattress, 3 blankets and a coverlet

A set of combs and clothes-brushes

A set of tooth-brushes and tooth-powder

A set of shoe-brushes and 12 cakes of blacking or
½ doz. bottles of ditto

A pewter wash-hand basin and a pewter cup

A strong sea-chest with a till and 2 trays in it, and a
good lock with 2 keys

A quadrant and a small day and night glass

A silver table-spoon and tea-spoon

A knife and fork, and a pocket-knife and penknife

A log-book and journal with paper, pens and ink

Robinson's *Elements of Navigation*

The Requisite Tables and Nautical Almanac

Bible, prayer-book

When going on a foreign station, an additional
dress-suit, with more light waistcoats, a cocked
hat, and some additional linen.

He reports his presence to the officer of the watch
and he is taken to the midshipmen's berth: this is likely
to be something of a shock to him, since it is a dank,
smelly, cheerless hole with no light or air and precious
little in the way of food or comfort, very far down in

the ship. The midshipmen's berth: but he is not a mid-shipman – far from it. He is rated first-class volunteer if there is room for one on the ship's books, or captain's servant or even able seaman if there is not, and he will not become a real midshipman for a couple of years. But he does not black the captain's boots, of course, nor attempt an able seaman's duties; he and all like him are called 'the young gentlemen' and he wears a midshipman's uniform (blue coat with a white patch on the collar, white breeches and cocked hat for formal occasions, otherwise blue jacket with blue or white trousers and a top hat, and a sword or dirk). Above all, he walks the quarterdeck, the officers' preserve. He has to walk it for six years, learning his duty aloft and on deck, going to the ship's schoolmaster in the mornings for mathematics and navigation, and keeping his official journal; and all this time, whether he is captain's servant, midshipman or master's mate (a senior midshipman) he is in fact only a rating, liable to be disrated at his captain's pleasure or even turned ashore; and if he behaves badly he can be punished, often being sent to the mast-head to spend several hours there, repenting of his sins.

At the end of his six years at sea he goes to the Navy Office, bearing certificates of competence and good behaviour from his captains, his journals, and perhaps a paper to say he is twenty. In theory this was the minimum age for a lieutenant, but in fact there were some of fifteen and sixteen. Six years on the ship's books, two of them as a midshipman, was insisted upon, however.

So here he is at the Navy Office with a trembling heart, trying to remember the difference between port and starboard; and here they put him through an oral examination in seamanship and navigation. He is not a booby: he has learnt a good deal in his six years afloat; and he gets through. He has 'passed for lieutenant'! He is charmed, delighted, but still very anxious; for it is one thing to pass and quite another to be given the precious commission. However, he has done well at sea, his captains speak well of him, his family has some influence in politics or at the Admiralty, band one day there arrives a beautiful piece of paper covered with official seals and signatures, reading:

By the Commissioners for executing the Office of Lord High Admiral of Great Britain and Ireland &c and of all His Majesty's Plantations &c

To Lieutenant William Blockhead, hereby appointed Lieutenant of His Majesty's Ship the Thunderer

By Virtue of the Power and Authority to us given We do hereby constitute and appoint you Lieutenant of His Majesty's Ship the Thunderer, willing and requiring you forthwith to go on board ... Strictly charging and Commanding all the Officers and Company belonging to the said Thunderer subordinate to you to behave themselves jointly and severally ... with all due Respect and Obedience ... And you shall likewise to observe and execute ... what orders and directions ... you shall receive from your Captain or any other your superior Officers ... Hereof nor you nor any of you may fail as you will answer the contrary at your peril.

Now he is a real officer at last, with the King's commission. He comes down on his poor father for a splendid new uniform (a blue coat with white cuffs and white lapels reaching right down his front, white waistcoat and breeches for full dress to be worn on grand occasions, and a plainer blue coat, often worn with trousers or blue breeches, for ordinary wear). He hopes this will be the last time he will have to do so, for now he is earning no less than £5 12s 0d a month, and there is always the golden prospect of prize-money. His father hopes so too.

He joins the *Thunderer*, 74, his commission is solemnly read out to the ship's company, and he takes up his quarters in the ward-room, together with the other lieutenants, the Marine officers, the master, the surgeon, the chaplain and the purser; it is a handsome room in a 74, with plenty of air and light coming through the great stern window, and he even has a tiny cabin of his own. He forswears the squalor of the midshipmen's berth for ever and settles down to his new duties. The years go by; and usually he moves from ship to ship, gaining a great deal of experience. He becomes more and more senior on the lieutenants' list as his elders are killed or promoted, and in time he is first lieutenant, no longer keeping a watch but responsible for the day-to-day running of the ship, her discipline and her appearance. He draws no extra pay, but he is next in line for promotion, and at last it comes – his ship distinguishes herself in battle and her first lieutenant is made master and commander. He leaves the *Thunderer* after a last splendid party, buys another uniform (a blue gold-laced coat and white breeches for full dress, the same coat and blue breeches for undress) and waits to be given a command of his own. This is another anxious period, for he knows very well that there are about four hundred commanders on the Navy List and no more than about a hundred sloops, the only vessels they can command.

And now, while he is waiting, stirring up all his

friends to use their influence, I will say something
about uniforms. It is a very curious fact, but before 1748
the Royal Navy had none at all: the officers wore what
they thought fit – often red coats, sometimes old tweed
breeches at sea, and any kind of hat that caught their
fancy. Then in that year uniform was laid down for
the officers, but it was not until 1857 that the men had
one – they fought the Battle of Trafalgar in anything
from petticoat breeches (a kind of depraved kilt dating
from the middle ages) to canvas trousers, with fur caps,
top hats or handkerchiefs on their heads, and jerseys
or chequered shirts; though most wore the purser's
slops, which were roughly of a pattern. But although
he had no uniform, the man-of-war's man could be
recognized at once, particularly when he was in his
shore-going rig: this usually consisted of a shiny black
glazed tarpaulin hat (hence Jack Tar for a sailor) with
a long dangling ribbon embroidered with the name of
his ship, a bright blue jacket with gilt buttons down the
right side, very broad, loose trousers, white or blue, tiny
black shoes with bows or silver buckles, a shirt, white,
spotted, striped or coloured, open at the collar, and
black silk handkerchief loosely knotted round the neck,
and a long scarlet waistcoat, the whole decorated with
ribbons at the seams, for glory. As well as this he often
had little gold earrings and a long swinging pigtail

(those whose hair did not grow would sometimes eke it out with oakum), so that there was no mistaking the man-of-war's man, particularly as he chewed his tobacco rather than smoking it like a Christian. I will also say something about sloops. Rightly speaking, a sloop is and always was a one-masted fore-and-aft vessel; but the Admiralty extended the term to cover ships and other craft that could be commanded by a master and commander, so that when a man-of-war brig had a lieutenant as her captain she was a brig (with two masts), but the moment a commander took her over she became a mere sloop, to the unspeakable amazement of landsmen.

Our young commander was born lucky. He has his sloop in a month or two – she takes a French corvette of equal force and he is promoted again. He is posted into a frigate, for he is now a post-captain. As a commander he was called Captain Blockhead by courtesy, and of course he was the captain of his ship; but now he is a full-blown captain and he is so addressed in official letters by the Admiralty. This time he does not have to buy a new uniform: his old coat will do, and all that is needed is to shift his epaulette from his left shoulder to his right, with the comforting reflection (if his promotion is before 1812) that when he is a captain of three years' seniority he will wear two, one on each shoulder, and the even more comforting reflection that from now on his promotion is automatic. Many of his former shipmates have stuck at lieutenant, many at commander, but the post-captains move steadily up the list, and now nothing but death or very shocking misconduct will prevent him from being an admiral at last. After some years in frigates he is given a ship of the line, and slowly he climbs the captains' list until at last he is at the top. The oldest of all the full admirals dies, and every-one moves up a step – our post-captain is made a rear-admiral! There is one last anxiety in his mind, however: he may be given no flag – he may be only a 'yellow admiral', condemned to live the rest of his life ashore on half-pay. But his luck still holds, and not only is he made rear-admiral of the blue but he is given a squadron to command. He goes aboard his flagship, hoists his blue ensign at the mizen; the squadron salutes it with thirteen guns and they proceed to sea. (The Navy never *goes*: it always *proceeds*.) But however well he fights it makes no difference to his promotion. He moves up the flag-list automatically – no one can get ahead of him and he cannot get ahead of anyone else, no matter what victories he may win. Rear-admiral of the blue, of the white, of the red. (In the seventeenth century, when very numerous fleets were engaged in the Dutch wars, the British fleets were divided into three squadrons, the red in the centre, the white in the van and the blue in the rear; and each squadron had its own admiral, vice-admiral and rear-admiral, the admiral of the red squadron being the admiral of the fleet.) Then vice-admiral of the blue, the white, hoisting his white ensign at the fore (this was the highest rank that Nelson ever reached), and of the red. Then admiral, full admiral: and at last, an old, old, very old man, he hoists the union flag at the main, for he is the most senior of them all, the admiral of the fleet.

I have spoken of other officers in the ward-room, the master, the surgeon and the purser: they messed in the ward-room and they had the right to walk the quarterdeck, but they were not commissioned officers – they held a warrant from the Navy Office and they never had quite the standing of the others. The master was a relic from the times when sailors sailed the ships and soldiers did the fighting, and he was still responsible for the navigation; he usually began as a midshipman, became a master's mate, and then, having few social advantages and no influence, gave up all hope of a commission, accepted a warrant and so reached the highest rank that he was ever likely to attain. The surgeon was the ship's medical man, of course; and the purser looked after the ship's provisions and the slops, or clothes that were sold to the men at sea; he had almost nothing to do with pay. The purser was not often a popular officer, and 'pusser's tricks' meant any kind of swindle with food, drink, tobacco and clothes, the most notorious being 'purser's eights', or his habit of receiving food at sixteen ounces to the pound and serving it out at fourteen, keeping the odd two for himself.

There were other warrant officers, such as the boatswain, who looked after the rigging, sails, anchors, cables and cordage, and who hurried the men to their duty, and the gunner and the carpenter, who were of great importance in the life of the ship: they usually rose from the lower deck, and they messed by themselves, not in the ward-room.

The lower deck itself was made up of the great mass of the ship's people – all the ratings from boy, third class (the lowest form of marine life) to able seaman. The captain appointed the petty officers such as the quartermasters, ship's corporal, boatswain's mate and so on from among them, but it made little difference to their sense of being the same kind of men. They nearly all lived and messed together on the lower deck between the guns, slinging their hammocks from the low beams overhead. They were allowed fourteen inches a man, but as they were divided into two watches, larboard and starboard, each on duty in turn, they usually had the luxury of twenty-eight inches to lie in: some 500 men packed into a space about 150 feet long and 50 at the widest. Their life was very hard, often dangerous, and always ill-paid; what is more, their meagre pay was invariably kept six months in arrears, in the hope that this would prevent them from running away. If their food had been good in the first place and if it had been honestly served out and decently cooked, it would not have been too bad by the standards of the time; but generally this was not the case. Indeed, it was usually so bad that when they could catch them, the men often ate rats, or millers as they were called in the service, because of their dusty coats as they got into the flour and dried peas. They were neatly skinned and cleaned and laid out for sale: hungry midshipmen would buy them too, and Admiral Raigersfeld, looking back on his youth, says, 'They were full as good as rabbits, although not so large.' Speaking of the bread he observes, 'The biscuit that was served to the ship's company was so light, that when you tipped it upon the table, it almost fell into dust, and thereout numerous insects, called weevils, crawled; they were bitter to the taste, and a sure indication that the biscuit had lost its nutritious particles; if instead of these weevils, large white maggots with black heads made their appearance (these were called bargemen in the Navy), then the biscuit was considered to be only in its first state of decay; these maggots were fat and cold to the taste, but not bitter.'

Here is a list of the provisions that were usually served out:

SUNDAY, 1 lb of biscuit, 1 lb of salt pork, half a pint of dried peas.

MONDAY, 1 lb of biscuit, half a pint of oatmeal, 2 oz of sugar and butter, 4 oz of cheese.

TUESDAY, 1 lb of biscuit, 2 lb of salt beef.

WEDNESDAY, 1 lb of biscuit, half a pint of peas and oatmeal, 2 oz of butter and sugar.

THURSDAY, 1 lb of biscuit, 1 lb of pork, half a pint of peas, 4 oz of cheese.

FRIDAY, 1 lb of biscuit, half a pint of peas and oatmeal, sugar, butter and cheese as before.

SATURDAY, 1 lb of biscuit and 2 lb of beef.

When beer was to be had, they were given a gallon a day; when it was not, which was most of the time, they had their beloved grog. This was rum, mixed with three times the amount of water and a little lemon-juice against scurvy: they were given a pint of grog at dinner time and another for supper, and they often got dead drunk, particularly when they saved up their rations and drank it all at once.

They were nearly always uneducated, often unable to read or write, and they had generally lived very hard all their lives; but there were some wonderful men among them, brave, very highly skilled at their calling, magnificently loyal to their shipmates and to their officers if they were well led. As Nelson said, 'Aft the more honour, forward the better man.' By aft he meant the quarterdeck, abaft the mainmast, the officers' part of the ship, and by forward he meant the men, the foremast jacks, who lived forward of the mainmast.

They were brought together partly by free entry (popular officers like Saumarez or Cochrane could always man their ships with volunteers) and partly by the press-gang. Impressment was a rough and ready form of conscription, and the idea was that seamen should be taken from merchant ships or seized on land and compelled to serve in the fleet for as long as their services were required. In practice it meant that a short-handed ship (and a man-of-war needed an enormous crew – roughly ten times the size of a merchantman's) would send an officer ashore with a strong party of powerful, reliable sailors armed with pistols and cutlasses for show and clubs for use to catch any reasonably able-bodied man they could lay their hands on – seamen for choice but anyone who could haul on a rope if sailors were not to be found. There was also the impress service itself, where shore-based officers did much the same, sending their prey to receiving ships, whence they were drafted to the men-of-war. Then, in 1795, there was the quota-system, by which each county was required to provide so many men for the Navy. The counties responded by getting rid of their undesirables – thieves, poachers, paupers, general nuisances, nearly all of them landsmen, or as the men-of-war's men called them, grass-combing lubbers.

Faced with recruits of this kind, some of them straight from gaol, many officers tightened the already severe discipline of their ships: flogging became more frequent and more savage, and 'starting', hitting people with a cane or a rope's end, to make them jump to their work, grew far worse. The real seamen came in for a good deal of this, and they began to feel even more ill-used, particularly as these alleged volunteers, who were sometimes given the choice between transportation and the Navy, received a bounty of as much as £70 – well over four years' pay for an able seaman. The sailors were ill-used, they were knocked about, they were not paid at all when they were sick or wounded and off duty, their pay was always in arrears, they were allowed almost no shore-leave at home, and they were cheated out of their rations. At Spithead in 1797 they mutinied. This was a very important mutiny, not like the small though sometimes bloody outbreaks against a tyrannical brute of a captain: the men refused to take the fleet to sea unless their grievances were put right. They were extraordinarily moderate, merely petitioning the Admiralty, in the most respectful terms, for an increase in pay to bring their nineteen shillings a month up to the soldier's shilling a day, that their pound of provisions should be sixteen ounces, that fresh vegetables, instead of flour, should be served out when they were in port, and that they might be allowed a short leave to visit their families. They said they should certainly take their ships to sea if the French fleet came out; but until then they should stand by their demands. Nelson, among other officers, stated that 'his heart was with them' and that he was against 'the infernal system' of paying them by ticket rather than cash, so that they often had to leave their families penniless for years. In the end the Admiralty gave way; a bill was hurried through parliament, the mutineers were given the King's pardon, and they carried Lord Howe, the admiral who had conducted the negotiations, shoulderhigh through the streets of Portsmouth.

Before giving a table showing the pay of the Navy after these improvements and after some rises for the officers too, I will quickly run through the stations and duties of the crew. The older, most highly skilled able seamen were stationed on the forecastle; they were called sheet-anchor or forecastle-men, and there would be about 45 of them in a 74. Then came the topmen, all able seamen, but young and active, since all the duty above the lower yards fell to them: counting fore, main and mizen topmen, there would be 114 altogether. Then came the afterguard, mostly ordinary seamen and landmen, who worked the after-braces, main, mizen and lower stay-sails: they would number about 60. Lowest of all in public esteem were the waisters, a numerous body (115) of landmen and other poor creatures stationed in the waist to look after the main and fore sheets and do all the dirty, unskilled work that was going. Then there were the quartermasters, old, reliable seamen who conned the ship, directing the helmsman; and the quarter-gunners, each of whom had charge of four guns. Last there were the idlers, or people who did not keep a watch but only worked from dawn till eight at night, such as the master-at-arms, the cook, the sailmaker, the barber and so on.

PAY (PER LUNAR MONTH – THERE ARE 13 LUNAR MONTHS IN A YEAR)

Admiral of the Fleet	140	0	0	
Admiral	98	0	0	
Vice-Admiral	70	0	0	
Rear-Admiral	49	0	0	
Captain (of a first rate)	32	4	0	*down to 16 16 0 in a 6th rate*
Master and Commander	16	16	0	
Lieutenant	8	8	0	
Master (1st rate)	12	12	0	*down to 7 7 0 in a 6th rate*
Boatswain, gunner, purser	4	16	0	*down to 3 1 0 in a 6th rate*
Carpenter	5	16	0	*down to 4 16 0 in a 6th rate*
Master's mate	3	16	6	*down to 2 12 6 in a 6th rate*
Midshipman	2	15	6	*down to 2 0 6 in a 6th rate*
Chaplain	11	10	9¼ *(plus £5 a year from each mid-shipman and 1st class volunteer, and £20 a year for doing the duty of a schoolmaster)*

Able seaman	1	13	6	
Ordinary seaman	1	5	6	
Landman	1	2	6	
Boy (1st class)	9	0	0	a year
Boy (2nd class)	8	0	0	a year
Boy (3rd class)	7	0	0	a year

Armourer, 2.4.3, master-at-arms, 2.0.6, carpenter's mate 2.10.6, caulker and ropemaker 2.10.6, quartermaster and boatswain's mate 2.5.6, sailmaker and cooper 2.5.6 (1st rate) 2.0.6 (6th), gunners' mate 2.2.6, yeoman of the powder-room 2.0.6, caulker's mate 2.6.6, yeoman of the sheets 2.2.6 (1st rate) 1.16.6 (6th rate), captains of the forecastle, tops and afterguard 2.0.6 (1st rate) 1.16.6 (6th).

Life at Sea

Officially the ship's day ran from noon to noon, but to most of those aboard it seemed to begin about dawn or earlier, just before eight bells in the middle watch, or 4 a.m., when the boatswain's mates piped 'All hands' down the fore and main hatchways and hurried below roaring 'Larboard watch ahoy! Rise and shine. Show a leg there! Out or down, out or down. Rouse out, you sleepers,' and cutting down the hammocks of those who preferred to stay in bed, having had no more than four hours of sleep.

The business of the ship, when at sea, had to go on right round the clock, naturally, since she could not be tied up to a post for the night; and to deal with this situation the ship's company was divided into two watches, larboard (or port) and starboard, and the 24 hours were cut into seven periods of duty, also called watches, thus:

AFTERNOON WATCH	Noon to 4 p.m.
FIRST DOG-WATCH	4 p.m. to 6 p.m.
LAST DOG-WATCH	6 p.m. to 8 p.m.
FIRST WATCH	8 p.m. to midnight
MIDDLE WATCH	midnight to 4 a.m.
MORNING WATCH	4 a.m. to 8 a.m.
FORENOON WATCH	8 a.m. to noon

The odd number of watches meant that the night duty was fairly shared: the larboard watch would turn out at midnight one day and the starboard the next. But the two-watch system also meant that most of the men never had more than four hours' sleep at a time. The officers were divided into three watches, which gave them longer in bed, but on the other hand they were never allowed to sleep on duty whereas in calm weather the men who were not at the wheel or looking out might drowse in most ships when there was nothing to be done. The passage of time was marked by strokes on the ship's bell, one stroke for every half hour: so eight bells meant the end of the ordinary watch. And at every stroke the log was heaved, the speed of the ship and her course marked on the log-board, and the depth of water in the well reported by the carpenter or one of his mates, while at night all the sentinels called 'All's well.'

To go back to eight bells in the middle watch: as they were struck, so the watch that had been sleeping, the larboard watch, let us say, was mustered and the watch on duty dismissed to get what sleep they could before hammocks were piped up. About this time the idlers or day-men were called, and at two bells the decks were cleaned, first being wetted, then sprinkled with sand, then scrubbed with holy-stones great and small, then brushed, and lastly dried with swabs. This took until six bells, and at seven bells hammocks were piped up. Each man took his hammock (it had a number on it, corresponding with the number on the beam where it was slung), rolled it into a tight cylinder and brought it up on deck, where the quartermasters stowed them in the hammock-nettings along the sides: this aired the bedding after the awful fug below, provided some protection in case of battle (a hammock would stop a musket-ball and deaden a cannon-ball), and cleared the lower deck for cleaning.

At eight bells in the morning watch hands were piped to breakfast, which was biscuit, burgoo (a kind of milkless porridge) and, in some ships, cocoa. Half an hour was allowed for this feast. Now it was the forenoon watch and the starboard men were on duty again (the two watches were often called the larbowlines and starbowlines). The watch below cleaned the lower deck, with water if the weather was fine and the ports could be opened to dry the planks, otherwise with dry sand, holystones and brooms; then they might be allowed to rest, but some captains preferred them to exercise the great guns or to practise reefing topsails.

At eight bells in the forenoon watch the officers took the noon observations of the sun to fix the ship's position, the watch was changed and all hands piped to dinner. The men divided themselves into messes, usually of eight friends, and one of the eight was appointed their cook for the day: he received the mess's ration from the ship's cook in the galley, saw to its dressing and brought it to his messmates as they sat at their hanging table between the guns. It took about half an hour to eat, and then at one bell the fifer on the main deck began to play 'Nancy Dawson' or some other tune that meant the grog was ready. The cooks darted up the ladder with little tubs or blackjacks to the butt where the master's mate had publicly mixed the rum, water and lemon-juice. He served it out with great care, and with great care the cooks carried it down, while their messmates banged their plates and cheered. It was shared out, but in tots slightly smaller than the tot the officer had used, so that a little was left over: this was called the cook's plush, and he drank it as a reward for his trouble.

At two bells dinner was over: the larbowlines were on duty, and generally the starbowlines were turned up as well for exercise. At six bells in the afternoon watch, or 4 p.m., hands were piped to supper, which was much the same as breakfast, but with another issue of grog. Supper took half an hour; by this time it was one bell in the first dog-watch, and a little later the drum beat to quarters. All hands hurried to their action-stations and the guns were cast loose. The midshipmen and then the lieutenants inspected the men under their charge and eventually the first lieutenant, having received their reports, reported 'All present and sober, sir, if you please,' to the captain, who would then have the guns run in and out and perhaps fired, or topsails reefed or furled and loosed.

When this was over the drum beat the retreat, hammocks were piped down, and at eight bells the watch was set. The larboard watch went below, straight to sleep; lights were put out on the lower deck, and the starboard watch took up its duty. At eight bells the larbowlines were called again for the middle watch, and four hours later, towards dawn, the day began again with the cleaning of the decks, this time by the starboard watch.

As you see, the men had at the most four hours of sleep one night and seven the next, with what they might snatch during the day. But in any emergency, such as reducing sail in dirty weather or tacking ship, or the least hint of action, all hands would be called and the watch below tumbled up, perhaps with no sleep at all.

This was an ordinary ship's day; but on others the routine changed, particularly on Thursdays and Sundays. On Thursdays hammocks were piped up at 4 a.m.; the hands spent the morning washing their clothes and the afternoon making and mending them. On Sundays hammocks were piped up at six bells and breakfast was at seven bells; then the ship and everything in her was brought to a high state of perfection, the men washed, shaved and put on their clean good clothes; they combed and plaited one another's pigtails, and at five bells in the morning watch they were mustered by divisions, the lieutenant of each division inspecting them as they stood in lines, toeing one particular seam on the deck. Then the captain, having inspected them too, went right round the ship with the first lieutenant to see that everything, including the cook's great coppers, was spotless. It usually was, but if he found anything dirty or out of order, then there would be the very devil to pay. After the captain's inspection there was a service on the quarterdeck, conducted by the chaplain if the ship carried one and by the captain if she did not. Some captains would preach a sermon, but others merely read out the Articles of War.

Then the men were piped to dinner, which might include such delights as figgy-dowdy, made by putting ship's biscuits into a canvas bag, pounding them with a marlinspike, adding bits of fat, figs and raisins, and boiling the whole in a cloth. Until supper-time they were as free as the work of the ship allowed. If they were in company with other ships or in port they would often go ship-visiting; or the liberty-men might be allowed on shore, especially in such places as Malta or Gibraltar, where it was easy to catch them if they tried to desert. After supper they were mustered, each man passing in front of the captain as his name was called and checked off on the ship's books: and when the muster was over it was time for quarters again.

Some ships had special days for punishment; others might punish all round the week. It always took place at six bells in the forenoon watch. The boatswain's mates piped 'All hands to witness punishment' and the men flocked aft, where the Marines were drawn up with their muskets on the poop and all the officers were present in formal dress, wearing their swords. The master-at-arms brought his charges before the captain and the misconduct of which they were accused (usually drunkenness) was publicly stated. If the man had anything to say for himself he might do so, and if any of his particular officers saw fit they might put in a word for him. Having considered the case, the captain gave his decision – acquittal, reprimand or punishment. This might be extra duties or stoppage of grog, but often it was flogging. 'Strip,' the captain would say, and the seaman's shirt came off. 'Seize him up,' and the quartermasters tied his hands to a grating rigged for the purpose upright against the break of the poop, reporting, 'Seized up, sir.' Then the captain read the Articles of War that covered the offence, he and all the others taking off their hats as he did so. He said, 'Do your duty,' and a boatswain's mate, taking the cat-of-nine-tails out of a red baize bag, laid on the number of strokes awarded. Some hands screamed, but the regular man-of-war's man would take a dozen in silence.

It was a vile, barbarous business by our standards, and an ugly one even by the more brutal standards of the time – no women were allowed to witness it. Many captains, Nelson and Collingwood among them, hated flogging, and there were ships that kept excellent taut discipline without bringing the cat out of the bag for months on end; but there were other captains, such as the infamous Pigot of the *Hermione* whose crew eventually hacked him to pieces off the Spanish Main, who rigged the grating almost every day and whose sentences, instead of Collingwood's six, nine or at the most twelve strokes, actually ran into the hundreds.

These men were despised by their fellow-officers, not only for being inhuman brutes but for being inefficient brutes into the bargain. A happy ship was the only excellent fighting-machine – a ship whose well-trained, well-led crew would follow their officers anywhere, a ship that would fight like a tiger when she came into action.

Action was the goal of every sea-officer; and when it came, how a ship sprang to life! The drum beat to quarters, the men raced to their familiar stations and cast loose their guns, the officers' cabins disappeared, the thin bulkheads, the furniture and all lumber vanishing into the hold to give a clear sweep fore and aft, the decks were wetted and sanded against fire. Damp cloth screens appeared around the hatches; in the magazines the gunner and his mates served out powder to the boys with their cartridge-cases; the yards were secured with chains; the galley fires were put out; and all this happened in a matter of minutes.

If it was a fleet action the captain and his first lieutenant on the quarterdeck would have their eyes on the admiral or the repeating frigates almost as much as on the enemy, for it was of the first importance to follow the admiral's signals. The traditional fleet action was begun with both sides manoeuvring for the weather-gage – that is, trying to gain a position to windward of the enemy so as to have the advantage of forcing an engagement at the right moment. Then the two fleets would form their line of battle, usually with about four hundred yards between the ships in each line to allow for change of course; and the idea was that each captain should engage his opposite number on the other side. The Fighting Instructions insisted that the battle-line should be rigidly maintained, and any captain who strayed from it was liable to be court-martialled: he must keep his station, and, since those who were not next to the admiral in this straight line could not see his signals because of the sails of the next ahead or astern, they had to watch the frigates (which always lay outside the line) whose duty it was to repeat the flagship's orders.

But these battles rarely led to a decisive result, and in 1782 in the West Indies, Rodney disobeyed the Instructions, broke the French line and captured the enemy flagship and five others. In the war that began in 1793 nearly all the great fleet actions disregarded official tactics. "Never mind manoeuvres," said Nelson. "Always go at them." This he did at Saint Vincent, the Nile and Trafalgar, just as Duncan did at Camperdown: after the first formal approach the fleet action quickly became a wild free-for-all in which better gunnery and seamanship won the day. At St Vincent, for example, Sir John Jervis, with Nelson under his orders and fifteen ships of the line, took on a Spanish fleet of 27, including seven first rates, captured four and beat the rest into a cocked hat.

Another and more frequent sort of action was that fought between frigates, sometimes in small squadrons but more often as single ships; and in these everything depended on the captain – he fought his ship alone. One of the finest was the battle between HMS *Amethyst*, 36, and the French *Thétis*, 40. Late on a November evening in 1808, close in with the coast of Brittany, Captain Seymour caught sight of the *Thétis* slipping out of Lorient with an east-north-east wind, bound for Martinique. He at once wore in chase, and by cracking on sail he came up with her by about 9 p.m., although she was a flyer. The *Thétis*, running a good nine knots, suddenly shortened sail and luffed up, turning to rake the *Amethyst* with all her broadside guns. The *Amethyst* was having none of that: she swerved violently to port and then, the moment the French broadside was fired, to starboard, shooting up into the wind just abreast of the *Thétis*. And now began a furious cannonade, both ships battering one another at close range as fast as they could load and

fire. The *Thétis*, as well as her extra guns, had 100 soldiers aboard, and they joined in with their musketry:
the din was prodigious. After half an hour, when the
Amethyst was a little ahead, the *Thétis* tried to cross
under her stern and rake her, but there was not room
and she ran her bowsprit into the *Amethyst*'s rigging
amidships: in a few moments they fell apart, and still
running before the wind they continued to hammer
one another like furies. After another half hour of
this the *Amethyst* forged ahead, put her helm hard
a-starboard, crossed the *Thétis*' hawse and raked her,
the whole broadside sweeping the Frenchman's deck
from stem to stern. Again they ran side by side, lighting
up the night with their incessant fire; but at 10.20 the
Amethyst's mizenmast came down, smashing the wheel
and sprawling over her quarterdeck. The *Thétis* shot
ahead, meaning to cross and rake the *Amethyst* in her
turn. But before she could do so, her own mizen went
by the board. Once more the frigates were side by side,
each hammering the other with a murderous fire. At
11 the *Thétis* had had enough: she steered straight for
the *Amethyst* to board her. Captain Seymour saw that
they would collide bow to bow and that the rebound
would bring their quarters together. He gave the order
not to fire. The ships struck, sprang apart, and then
just before the Frenchman's quarter swung against the

Amethyst he cried 'Fire!' and the whole broadside tore into the *Thétis*' boarders as they stood ready to spring from her quarterdeck. She could only reply with 4 guns, and a moment later the ships were locked together, the *Amethyst*'s best bower anchor hooked into the *Thétis*' deck. So they lay for another hour and more, their guns still blazing furiously. The *Thétis* was set alight in many places, her fire gradually slackened, and at twenty minutes after midnight Captain Seymour called 'Boarders away!', leapt aboard with his men and carried her at the point of the sword. A little later the Frenchman's two remaining masts fell over the side. Her hull was terribly shattered, and in her very courageous resistance she had lost 135 killed, including her captain, and 102 wounded. The *Amethyst* lost 19 killed and 51 wounded.

The comparative strength of the two frigates:

	Amethyst	*Thétis*
Broadside guns	21	22
broadside weight of metal	467 lb	524lb
crew	261	436 (counting the 106 soldiers)
size	1046 tons	1090 tons

The rewards of victory were very great. The successful sea-officer enjoyed an honour, glory and popularity that no other man could earn. And after the great fleet actions the admirals were given peerages, huge presents of money and pensions of thousands a year; the victorious frigate-captain was made a baronet; first lieutenants were promoted commander and some midshipmen were given their commissions; but apart from public praise the rewards did not usually go much lower than that. For tangible advantages the ship's company looked to something else – to prize-money.

Whenever a man-of-war captured an enemy ship and brought her home she was first condemned as lawful prize and then sold. The proceedings were shared thus:

	before 1808	after 1808
Captain	3/8	2/8
Lieutenants, master, captain of Marines, equal shares of	1/8	1/8
Marine lieutenants, surgeon, purser, boatswain, gunner,carpenter, master's mates, chaplain, equal shares of	1/8	1/8

Midshipmen, lower warrant officers, gunner's, boatswain's and carpenter's mates, Marine sergeants, equal shares of	⅛	4/8
Everybody else, equal shares of	2/8	

Before 1808 the captain had to give one of his eighths to the flag-officers under whose orders he served: after 1808, one third of what he received. If he were not under an admiral he kept it all in both cases.

From the point of view of mere lucre, leaving honour and glory aside, it was not very profitable to take an enemy man-of-war: she was usually shockingly battered by the time she surrendered, and in any case she carried nothing but a cargo of cannon-balls and guns. To be sure, there was head-money of five pounds for every member of her crew, but real wealth, real splendid wealth, came only from the merchant or the treasure ship, laden with silk and spice, or, even more to the point, with gold and silver. An East-Indiaman was worth a fortune, and a ship from the Guinea coast, laden with gold-dust and elephants' teeth, meant dignified ease for life.

Back in 1743, when Anson, having rounded the Horn, having survived incredible hardships, and having sailed right across the Pacific, took the great Manilla galleon, he found 1,313,842 pieces of eight aboard her, to say nothing of the unminted silver. He brought it home, and 32 wagons were needed to carry it to the Tower of London: even a boatswain's mate had well over a thousand guineas for his share, while Anson, an admiral and a peer of the realm, was a very wealthy man.

And in 1762, when it became clear that a war with Spain was inevitable, cruisers were sent out: two of them, the *Active*, 28, and the *Favourite*, 20, had information of a register ship from Lima to Cadiz. As Beatson, the contemporary historian, says, they 'had the good fortune to get sight of her on the 21st of May, and immediately gave chase. In a few hours they were close along-side, when Captain Sawyer hailed them whence they came; and, on being answered from Lima, he desired them to strike, for that hostilities were commenced between Great Britain and Spain. This was a piece of news they were not prepared for; but after a little hesitation, they submitted. Possession was then taken of the vessel, the *Hermione*, which was by far the richest prize made during the war; the cargo and ship, etc., amounting to £544,648 1s. 6d.'

This splendid cake was cut up thus:

To the admiral and commodore *Active*'s share	£64,963	3	9
captain	65,053	13	9
each commissioned officer	13,003	14	1
each warrant officer	4,336	3	2
each petty officer (this included midshipmen)	1,806	10	3
each seaman, etc.	485 5	4	¾

The *Favourite*'s share was £825 less, because she was not entitled to head-money for the 165 prisoners.

In 1804 much the same thing happened again: the Spaniards sent their treasure across the ocean, and off Cadiz there were four frigates of the Royal Navy waiting for it. It must be admitted that England had not formally declared war, but they took it just the same. This time there was a fight, the Spanish ships being frigates of their navy, and in the course of it one most unfortunately blew up. The other three struck, and they were found to be carrying 5,810,000 pieces of eight. However, the Admiralty in an odd fit of conscience, decided that this was not lawful prize (although the frigates had been ordered to go and take it) and that

the money, apart from a small proportion, should go
to the Crown; so in the end the poor captains had to
content themselves with a mere £15,000 apiece. Still,
seeing that the captain of a sixth rate then earned
just over £100 a year, they had made 150 years' pay in
a morning, just as the seamen of the *Active* had made
36 years' in an afternoon; and in any case, there might
always be another *Hermione* round the next headland.

There never was another *Hermione*; but splendid
prizes were still to be made, and the very real possibility of a fortune lying just over the horizon, to be
won by a bold stroke, a few hours' fierce action, added
a certain charm to the sailor's hard and dangerous life
at sea.

Songs

The beautiful working-songs and shanties of the merchant ships had no place in the Royal Navy, which was a silent service. But even so, there was music aboard a man-of-war: when the grog was served out the ship's fifer or fiddler played 'Nancy Dawson', or 'Sally in our Alley'; when the men were drummed to quarters it was to the tune of 'Heart of Oak'; and when the anchor was being weighed the fiddler sat on the capstan and struck up 'Drops of Brandy'. And then of course there were the songs and ballads the sailors sang, particularly on a Saturday night at sea. Here is one of the most popular of them:

Farewell and adieu to you fine Spanish ladies,
Farewell and adieu all you ladies of Spain,
For we've received orders to sail for old England
And perhaps we shall never more see you again.

   We'll rant and we'll roar like true British sailors,
   We'll range and we'll roam over all the salt seas,

Until we strike soundings in the Channel of old
    England –
From Ushant to Scilly 'tis thirty-five leagues.

We hove our ship to when the wind was sou'west, boys,
We hove our ship to for to strike soundings clear,
Then we filled our main-tops'l and bore right away, boys,
And right up the Channel our course we did steer.

    We'll rant and we'll roar, etc.

The first land we made is known as the Dodman,
Next Ram Head near Plymouth, Start, Portland and Wight;
We sailèd past Beachy, past Fairley and Dungeness,
And then bore away for the South Foreland light.

    We'll rant and we'll roar, etc.

Then the signal is made for the Grand Fleet to anchor
All all in the Downs that night for to meet,
So stand by your stoppers, see clear your shank-painters,
Haul all your clew-garnets, stick out tacks and sheets.

    We'll rant and we'll roar, etc.

Now let every man toss off a full bumper,
Now let every man toss off a full bowl,
For we will be jolly and drown melancholy
In a health to each jovial and true-hearted soul.

We'll rant and we'll roar, etc.

And here is part of a home-made ballad, one of the many composed and sung by sailors:

I'll tell you of a fight, boys, and how it did begin.
It was in Gibraltar Gut, which is nigh unto Apes' Hill;
It was three privateers that belonged unto Spain
Who thought our British courage for to stain.

I'll tell you, brother sailors: it was on a calm day,
Then one of the privateers they boarded us straightaway:
They hove in their powder-flasks and their stink-pots,
But we repaid them with our small shot.

They being in number three hundred and more,
And is not equal, you'll say, unto threescore:
But now I will tell you the courage of our men,
That we valued them not, if they had been ten.

Our small arms did rattle, and our great guns did roar,
Till one of them we sank, and the other run ashore;
Such a slaughter we made as you seldom shall see,
Till an hundred and eighty we drown'd in the sea.

Our fight being over, and our fray being done,
And every man then scowering his gun,
And every man to a full flowing bowl;
Here's a health to all British loyal souls.

My name is George Cook, the author of this,
And he may be hang'd that will take it amiss.

And here is another, about the action between *HMS Nymphe* and the French frigate *Cléopâtre* in June 1793:

Come, all you British heroes, listen to what I say;
'Tis of a noble battle that was fought the other day;
And such a sharp engagement we hardly ever knew:
Our officers were valiant and our sailors so true.

The La Nymphe was our frigate, and she carried a valiant
crew,
With thirty-six twelve-pounders, that made the French
to rue.
At daylight in the morning the French hove in sight;
Captain Pellew he commanded us in this fight.

Full forty eighteen-pounders we had for to engage;
The French they thought to confound us, they seemed so much
enrag'd.
Our captain cry'd, 'Be steady, boys, and well supply each gun;
We'll take this haughty Frenchman, or force her for to run!'

The action then began, my boys, with shot on every side;
They thought her weight of metal would soon subdue our
pride.

I think the second broadside her captain he was slain,
And many a valiant Frenchman upon the decks were lain.

We fought her with such fury, made every shot to tell,
And thirteen brave seamen in our ship there fell,
Tho' forty-five minutes was the time this fight did last,
The French ship lost her tiller and likewise her mizen mast.

Then yard arm and yard arm we by each other lay,
And sure such noble courage to each other did display;
We form'd a resolution to give the French a check,
And instantly we boarded her off the quarter-deck.

Her colours being struck, my boys, she then became our prize,
And our young ship's company subdued our enemies,
Altho' they were superior in metal and in men.
Of such engagements you may seldom hear again.

And now in Portsmouth Harbour our prize is safely moor'd.
Success to all brave sailors that enter now on board;
A health to Captain Pellew, and all his sailors bold,
Who value more their honour than misers do their gold.

Which is not a bad note on which to finish a short account of the Royal Navy of Nelson, St Vincent, Duncan, Howe, Cochrane, Seymour and a hundred thousand other true-hearted seamen.

Jack Aubrey's Ships

BRIAN LAVERY

Patrick O'Brian, unlike other writers of naval fiction, often uses real ships as the basis for his plots. In the Hornblower stories of C. S. Forester, for example, the hero serves on only one real ship – the *Indefatigable*, which really was the ship commanded by Captain Pellew during the time when the hero served under him as midshipman.

Several of the Aubrey stories are based on real incidents and use real ships: in particular, *The Mauritius Command*, is based on the real campaign in that area. The use of real ships which have a past adds to the effect of the story: the cutting out of the *Hermione* in the case of the *Surprise*, and the incident between the *Leopard* and the USS *Chesapeake* in 1807, which led to difficulties after Jack Aubrey's capture by the Americans in *The Fortune of War*.

The Royal Navy of Napoleonic Wars had nearly 1,000 ships at its peak in 1814. These were divided into six rates, according to size and gunpowder, with numerous smaller vessels which were unrated.

In general the rates were divided as follows:

First Rate	100 + guns	850 + men
Second Rate	90–98 guns	750 men
Third Rate	64–84 guns	500–700 men
Fourth Rate	50–60 guns	350–420 men
Fifth Rate	30–40 guns	215–294 men
Sixth Rate	20–28 guns	121–195 men

Unrated ships included sloops of 10–18 guns, brigs, bomb vessels, fire-ships, storeships, cutters, schooners, luggers, hospital ships, prison ships, and gunboats.

After service as a midshipman and lieutenant, a successful naval officer would expect to take command of a sloop, with the rank of Commander. After promotion to Post Captain, he would rise through ships of the different rates, perhaps reaching a third rate after seven to ten years in command of frigates. In the early stages, Jack Aubrey's career roughly conforms to this. As a commander he began in the tiny sloop *Sophie* and, after a period on the beach, he continued in the *Polychrest*. Following his promotion, Aubrey took temporary command of the 38-gun fifth rate, the *Lively*. This was rather a large ship for a newly promoted captain, but the command was temporary and the circumstances were exceptional. He then went to the *Surprise*, a sixth rate of 28 guns, a ship more appropriate to his seniority. His next ship was the *Boadicea*, a fifth rate of 38 guns. After that his career in frigates might have ended. With six or seven years of seniority he was offered the *Ajax*, a ship-of-the-line of 74 guns, but turned it down in order to go to sea more quickly in the *Leopard*, a 50-gun ship.

After this Aubrey's rise up the rates slows down considerably. Stephen Maturin's intelligence activities generally demand small ships, and Aubrey is certainly more at home in the single ship missions carried out by frigates, than service with the main fleet in a ship-of-the-line. His next command after the *Leopard* (apart from several ships as a virtual passenger) is the sloop *Ariel*. It is made quite clear that he is being given the ship because of 'a delicate, pressing piece of work that calls for a cool, experienced hand', and that it was 'fully understood that the command of the *Ariel* in no way represented the Board's estimate of Captain Aubrey's merits'; the ship was technically transformed from a sloop to a post ship by the mere fact of Aubrey taking command.[1]

In *The Ionian Mission* Aubrey's career briefly resumes a normal course, when he becomes captain of the *Worcester* of 74 guns. This however does not last for long and he soon returns to his old friend the *Surprise*. The association with this ship continues through the remaining books, even surviving his dismissal from the navy in *The Reverse of the Medal*.

Aubrey's first two ships, the *Sophie* and the *Polychrest*, were fictitious, and rather unusual vessels. The *Sophie* was described as 'almost the only quarterdeck brig in the service', and certainly such a deck, reaching from the stern to almost midships in a larger ship, was highly unusual in one so small. Formerly known as the *Vencejo*, she had been captured from the Spanish. She was old-fashioned in construction and fitting, and was regarded as rather slow. She was about 150 tons in burthen, which would have made her about 70 ft long on the gundeck. Her main armament consisted of 14 guns, apparently very light ones firing 4-pound shot, but Aubrey successfully applied to have two 12-pounders fitted as 'bow chasers', firing directly forward. As a brig she would have been fitted with two masts, both carrying square sails.[2]

The *Polychrest* was even more unusual. She had been designed to carry a secret weapon, later abandoned. She was double-ended, in that head and stern were alike. She apparently had a very shallow draught, as she had no hold. This was compensated for by the use of sliding keels, rather like those used by modern dinghies (and in fact a few vessels were built with such sliding keels, mostly to the design of Captain Shanck). Her armament of twenty-four 32-pounder carronades was a very heavy one for a ship of her size, but would only have been effective at short range. She was three masted, square-rigged, but was unusual in that she had two main topsail yards. She was 'the *Carpenter's Mistake*', 'a theorizing landsman's vessel ... built by a gang of rogues and jobbers'.[3]

The *Lively* is the first real ship we encounter, and she was a perfectly standard frigate of 38 guns. When Aubrey took up his acting command in the autumn of 1804 she was almost brand new, having been launched at Woolwich Dockyard in July. She was the first of a class of 15 ships, designed by Sir William Rule the Joint Surveyor of the Navy. She was of 1,076 tons, 154 ft 1 in. long on the gundeck, and 39ft 6in. broad. Like other ships of this type, she carried twenty-eight 18-pounder guns on the main deck, twelve 32-pounder carronades and two long 12-pounders on the quarterdeck, and two 32-pounder carronades and two long 9-pounders on the forecastle. Officially this type of ship carried a crew of 284 or 300 men, though in practice many were under-manned. By this time the 38 was the third most common type of frigate in the fleet. There were

45 of them on the list in 1805, compared with 53 frigates of 36-guns and 59 smaller vessels of 32-guns.

The *Surprise*, to which Aubrey was appointed after his temporary command of the *Lively* had ended, was 'a trim, beautiful little eight and twenty, French built with a bluff bow and lovely lines, weatherly, stiff, a fine sea boat, fast when she was well handled, roomy, dry'.[4] The real ship had distinguished herself in 1799. Two years earlier the crew of the frigate *Hermione*, under the brutal Captain Pigot, had mutinied and butchered their officers. They had surrendered her to the Spanish, who were fitting her out for their fleet at Puerto Cabello, in what is now Venezuela. On the night of 21 October six boats from the *Surprise* went into the enemy harbour, stormed the *Hermione* and towed her out to sea.[5]

The *Surprise* had been the French frigate *Unite*, built at Le Havre in 1794, and rated as a 'corvette' in the French Navy. In April 1796 she was captured by the 38-gun frigate *Inconstant* in the Mediterranean. She was renamed *Surprise*, because there was already a *Unite* in the British fleet, and registered as a 28-gun ship, though she actually carried twenty-four 32-pounder carronades on her main deck, and eight 32-pounder carronades on her quarterdeck and forecastle, with two or four long 6-pounders on the quarterdeck and forecastle. It was a very powerful armament for a frigate, but with remarkably few long-range guns. There was some difficulty about how to rate her – 28-guns normally meant a sixth rate, but she was regarded as fifth rate from 1797 to 1798 and as sixth rate for the rest of her career. She was only of 579 tons, but carried the mainmast of a 36-gun ship (normally of about 950 tons), with the foremast and mizzen of a 28. According to one authority, 'thus rigged, the *Surprise* appears not to have been complained of as a sailor.'[6]

She sailed for Jamaica in July 1796 under Captain Edward Hamilton and stayed in the West Indies for several years. She was involved in the capture of several privateers before her exploits with the *Hermione*, but returned home after that. Here reality departs from fiction. The real *Surprise* was sold at Deptford in February 1802 and presumably broken up. The short-lived Peace of Amiens had begun and the government believed it had no immediate need for such ships.

The fictional *Surprise* was to continue for many years, appearing in eight out of the fourteen Jack Aubrey novels published so far. It is worth describing her in some detail, both for herself and as a representative of ships of the period. In this we are helped by the fact that her plans, drawn by dockyard shipwrights

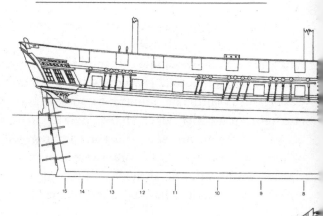

Profile of *H.M.S. Surprise*

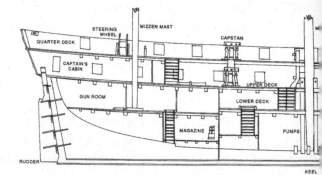

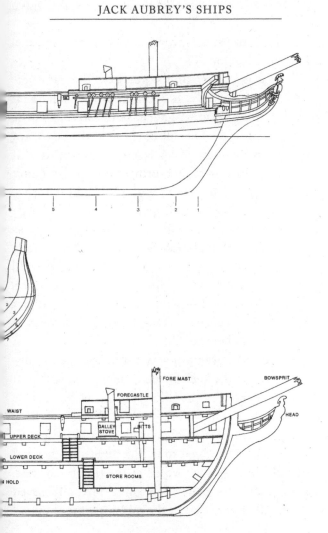

6   5   4   3   2   1

FORE MAST   BOWSPRIT

FORECASTLE   HEAD

WAIST

GALLEY
STOVE   BITTS

UPPER DECK

LOWER DECK

HOLD   STORE ROOMS

85

some time after her capture, survive in the National Maritime Museum.

She was 126ft long on the gundeck. This measurement did not give the full length of the ship, for it excluded the projecting gallery of the stern, and the figurehead and the knee of the head at the bows, not to mention the long projection of the bowsprit. But it was a useful way of measuring the ship, for it gave a real indication of the size of the hull, and the space that was available for fitting guns and accommodating men. At her widest point in midships she was 31ft 8in. broad, though under the planks she was only 31ft 2in. Using a standard formula, these figures could be used to calculate the tonnage of the ship, which was 578 73/94 tons. This gave no real indication of her weight or displacement, but was a useful comparison of her size with other warships.

The hull of a warship was a stout wooden structure. The straight keel formed the very lowest part and the backbone of the ship. At the forward end rose a curved piece, known as the stem. Aft rose a piece called the stern-post; this was made straight so that the rudder could be hinged to it. The three-dimensional shape of the ship was formed by the timbers, or ribs. Each of these was made up of several pieces of curved timber, called futtocks. In the midships, the ship had the characteristic 'tulip bulb' section, with a narrowing above the waterline known as 'tumblehome'. This was more pronounced on French ships than on British ones by this time, and is noticeable on the plans of the *Surprise*. At the bow and stern the structure was rather different. For most of the length of the ship the timbers ran across the keel, but at the bows they ran parallel to it – these were known as hawse pieces. Aft, horizontal timbers, called transoms, formed an essential part of the structure of the lower stern. Above the transoms, almost all ships of the time had a very weak structure pierced with windows. Aggressive captains like Jack Aubrey dreamed of 'raking' an enemy by firing their broad-side through these stern windows.

The timbers were covered by planks of varied thickness, both inside and outside. On the outside the thickest planks, known as wales, were fitted under the level of the decks. British ships of this period had single wales – those under the upper deck of a frigate would be about 7in. thick and 3ft 6in. deep. On a French ship like the *Surprise* the upper wales would be double, with two thick planks and thinner planks between them. The rest of the planking on a ship like the *Surprise* would be about 3in. thick. The underwater planks were covered by copper plates to protect the ship from weeds and shipworm.

In the hold the thicker planking, the thick stuff, was arranged to cover the places where the futtocks joined. Thick planks, called clamp, were also placed on the sides where they supported the decks. That between the gundecks was known as spirketting. The deck beams supporting the decks rested on the clamp. They were curved slightly upwards to give a camber which allowed water to drain to the scuppers in the sides of the ship. The beams were braced against the sides of the ship by L-shaped timbers known as knees. If fitted vertically, they were hanging knees; if horizontal, they were lodging knees. Between the deck beams were lighter timbers called carlines and ledges, and the plank of the deck was about two inches thick.

Like all frigates of the period, the *Surprise* had two complete decks running the full length of her hull. The lower deck was completely unarmed for it was just below the waterline – though perversely it was, for historical reasons, sometimes called the gundeck. It was used entirely for accommodation, with the men living forward of the mainmast and the officers aft, in an area known – equally perversely as the gunroom. The *Surprise* was slightly unusual, in that this deck was not continuous. About halfway between the mainmast and the mizzen it dropped by about a foot, thus increasing the headroom for the officers. Natural light and fresh air on the lower deck were minimal, coming in through gratings in the hatchways of the upper decks.

Above the lower deck was the upper or main deck. Each side of the ship was pierced with 12 gunports for firing the main armament so the upper deck had to be strong enough to support these guns which with carriage and fittings weighed about two tons each. The central part of the upper deck – known as the waist – was largely open and was therefore useless for accommodation. Forward, the upper deck was covered with a short deck known as the forecastle. Under that, on the fore part of the upper deck, was an iron stove used to prepare all the crew's provisions, and stout pieces of timber – known as the main bitts – used to fasten the cables when the ship was at anchor.

The after part of the upper deck, as far forward as the mainmast, was covered by the quarterdeck. Situated under that, right in the stern, was the captain's cabin. It had a row of windows aft to give good light. A quarter galley projected from each side, one of which was used as toilet accommodation for the captain. Forward of the captain's cabin was an open but covered area, used as shelter for the crew on watch.

It also included the lower part of the main capstan used for raising the anchor, lifting guns and other heavy duties. The heads of the ship's pumps were situated abreast of the mainmast. They reached down into the hold, and their most important duty was to empty the water from the lower part of the ship.

Both the quarterdeck and the forecastle carried guns; for reasons of stability, these were of lighter calibre than those on the upper deck. The quarterdeck of the *Surprise* appears to have had six guns and carronades per side, and the forecastle had two per side. The quarterdeck was fitted with the steering wheel and the binnacle containing the compass. It also had the upper part of the capstan. This was operated by putting a dozen bars into the holes in the 'drumhead'. Up to six men could push at each bar and the pressure of these men was used to haul at a rope wound round the drum. The quarterdeck was the main recreation area of the officers, but the crew had plenty of reasons to go there in the course of duty – for steering, operating the capstan, hauling on numerous rigging lines, or for working the guns.

The forecastle also served as the base for some rigging lines, mostly those associated with the foremast. It had a copper chimney for the galley stove on the upper deck, and it served as a station for much of the work to be done in raising the anchor.

The area under the lower deck was almost entirely devoted to storage. Right aft below the gunroom, the structure of the ship tended to rise and create an area slightly clearer of bilge water. This was the breadroom which was used to store the ship's biscuits. Just forward of that, still under the gunroom, was the magazine used to store powder in barrels and cartridges made up from paper or canvas. There was another small room forward of that, probably used for either alcoholic spirits or fish which were isolated from the rest of the provisions for reasons of security or smell.

The greatest part of the space under the lower deck made up the hold of the ship. Here the necessities of life – beef, pork, cheese, butter, peas, water and beer – were stored in wooden casks on top of iron or shingle ballast. In a sixth rate like the *Surprise*, the anchor cables, made of thick rope, were stored on planks placed on top of these casks.

Forward of the hold, three decks under the forecastle, were the warrant officer's stores where the bosun, the carpenter and the gunner kept supplies of timber, tar, blocks, rope, gun-carriage parts, tools, and hundreds of other items that were needed to keep the ship afloat and independent of the shore for months if necessary.

The *Surprise*, like all true 'ships', had three masts. The largest one – the main mast – was situated near the centre of the keep to give a balanced rig. The foremast was slightly smaller, and was placed just aft of the end of the keel. The mizzen mast was considerably smaller than the other two and was further from the stern than the foremast was from the bows, so that the gap between the fore and the main was very large. Each of the masts was made up of three sections. The lower part – the mast proper – passed through the decks to have its 'heel' fixed securely above the keel of the ship. As it passed through each deck it was secured by pieces of timber known as partners.

Above the mast were the topmast and the topgallant mast. Each overlapped slightly with the one below and was held close to it. At the head of the lower mast was a platform known as a top; at the head of the topmast were the 'cross trees'. Like the top, this too could serve as a base for the seamen working aloft and as posts for lookouts.

Forward of the hull, projecting at an angle of about 12 degrees from the horizontal, was a spar known as the bowsprit. It was extended by the jibboom and the flying jibboom in the same way that the masts were extended by topmasts and topgallants. The bowsprit could carry sails but its main function was to provide an anchorage for the rigging which supported the foremost from ahead.

Attached to the masts were the yards which spread

the sails. In general, there was one yard for each mast and this took its name from the mast – thus, for example, the mainmast had the main yard and the fore topmast had the fore topsail yard. The exception was the mizzen yard, which was for a fore and aft rather than a square sail. The foot of the mizzen topsail above needed a special yard – the crossjack – to extend it.

A ship like the *Surprise* needed about 30 miles of rope to support and control its sails and, apart from manning the guns in action, the operation and maintenance of it was the main task of the crew. The standing rigging supported the masts. It was thicker and stronger than the running rigging which controlled the sails and it was virtually fixed in position, except for maintenance purposes. It consisted of several types of rope. The stays supported the masts from ahead. The shrouds supported them from behind; the lower ones were fixed in 'channels' which projected from the ship's sides. Backstays went from the head of a topmast or topgallant to the channels, while 'futtock shrouds' supported the lower end of the backstays of the upper masts. Certain specialised ropes, such as gammoning and bobstays, kept the bowsprit in place against the upwards pull of the fore stays.

Even a relatively small ship carried more than an acre of sails. They came in two basic types. Square sails were the dominant ones on a ship and were so called because in their neutral position they hung square to the line of progress of the ship. Fore and aft sails, on the other hand, were fitted fore and aft when not in use. Square sails were ideal with the wind behind; fore and aft were best when trying to make way into the wind. The square sails were lashed to the yards, while the fore and aft sails, with the important exception of the mizzen course, were attached to the stays. All sails were made of strips of canvas sewed together, with rope sewed round them for strength. Reef-points were lines of rope fitted to certain sails, so that they could be reduced in area in a strong wind.

The running rigging was used to control the sails and it too consisted of many different types of rope: the braces controlled the angles of the yards with the wind; sheets controlled the lower corners of the sails; buntlines and clewlines were used to furl the sails; and bowlines were needed to hold the leading edge forward when sailing close to the wind.

The basic art of ship handling was to deploy the sails most effectively. Too much sail in a given wind would be dangerous and inefficient, so some sails would be furled, others reefed. In very light winds, light studding sails were used to extend the normal sails. The sails also had to be braced to the correct angle, at about 15 degrees to the apparent wind. No square-rigged ship could sail closer than six points, or 67 degrees to the wind, so a ship could only go directly to windward by zigzagging or 'beating to windward'.

Two basic manoeuvres were 'tacking' and 'wearing'. In the former, the ship was turned to bring the wind on her other side by turning her bows through the wind. The helm was put down to begin the turn and the sails on the main and mizzen mast were braced round to the opposite side. The foremast was kept in its original position to help the bows through the wind and then braced round too. Wearing was the opposite manoeuvre – the stern was turned to the wind. It was easier than tacking and the ship did not need as much speed to carry it out, but it took up more time and space. Another manoeuvre was 'heaving to' when the sails were adjusted to cancel each other out so that the ship was held almost stationary in the water without the use of anchors.

A ship of this period carried about four large anchors. Two of these anchors – the bowers – were in more or less permanent readiness in the bows. The other two – the sheet and the spare – were for emergency use. The anchors on the *Surprise* would have weighed about one and a half tons each.[7] She also had two much smaller anchors, the stream and the kedge, either of which could be slung under a boat, rowed forward, dropped and used to haul the ship forward when there was no wind. The cable of each anchor was of thick rope. It was hauled up by means of the ship's capstans. When not in use, the bower anchors were 'catted', that is they were hung from the catheads in the bows. They were also 'fished', in that their crowns, or pointed ends, were raised up to make the stock horizontal.

A 28-gun ship was allocated four boats. All could be rowed or sailed, but some were more suitable for one than the other. The 10-oared 28ft long barge was mainly for rowing the captain ashore or to other ships. The 28ft launch was the heaviest boat of the ship and was used for carrying stores. There were also two cutters – 24ft and 18ft long (the latter was often known as the jully boat). These boats were usually clinker-built, with overlapping planks. They were particularly good for sailing and were general purpose boats.[8]

A ship of this size would normally carry a crew of about 240 men, though on one occasion at least she is recorded as having 197 men.[9] She would have about 18 officers, including a captain, two lieutenants and the key warrant officers – the master, the surgeon, the purser, the gunner, the bosun and the carpenter – and four midshipmen. The rest of the men were the crew, or the 'lower deck'. They slept in hammocks and ate their simple meals at tables, sitting on wooden benches. Some were marines (about thirty in the case of the *Surprise*) while, in a strong crew, the bulk of the rest were experienced seamen rated 'able' or 'ordinary'. In a weaker crew there would be a large proportion of 'landsmen', adults who were unused to the sea.

This large group of men had to be divided into teams for all the various manoeuvres that the ship might carry out. There were two or three watches, so that the ship could be sailed and all except the most major evolutions carried out while part of the crew rested. Some men, such as servants and craftsmen, were known as 'idlers', and worked mainly in the daytime. Each watch was divided into six or so parts. The fore topmen, maintopmen and mizzen topmen worked up the masts and along the yards and included fit and skilled seamen. The forecastlemen, afterguard and waisters worked mainly on deck and were less skilled. The waisters, in particular, were the least skilled group of all. The marines might also be included in this organisation. A few were needed as sentries and wore full uniform, but most wore working clothing and helped the seamen about the decks. The organisation of the crew was the duty of the First Lieutenant, but Aubrey is professional enough to take a keen interest in the matter.

Aubrey is proud of the sailing qualities of the *Surprise*, and works hard to improve them. Catharpins, for example, are fitted to tighten the shrouds and allow the sails to be braced round further to catch the wind. He also has her restored to her original rig, with the mainmast of a 36-gun ship.[10] Apart from his own skills, Aubrey attributes the sailing qualities of the *Surprise* to her French build. In this he reflects the prejudices of sea officers of his time. Modern research tends to suggest that British ships, though slower than French ones in fair weather, were more robust and sailed better in storms and gales.

Aubrey's other ships can be dealt with more briefly. The *Boadicea* which features in *The Mauritius Command* was a real 38-gun frigate, built by Adams of Bucklers Hard in 1797. She was not broken up until 1858. The *Leopard*, the 'horrible old Leopard' of *Desolation Island* was a 50-gun ship launched, after long delays during her building, at Sheerness in 1790. Unlike the *Surprise* and other frigates, she had two complete decks of guns with an unarmed orlop deck below the waterline, a quarterdeck and forecastle. She was one of an obsolete type, too small to stand with larger ships in the line of battle and too slow to be an effective frigate. The *Java* and the *Shannon* of *The Fortune of War* were also real ships and their encounters with American vessels are accurately described. *La Fleche*, on the other hand, is fictitious.

The *Ariel* sloop of *The Surgeon's Mate* was evidently a real vessel, armed with sixteen 32-pounder carronades and two 9-pounders.[11] She was built in 1806 and survived ten years before being broken up at Deptford. This type of ship was essentially a scaled down frigate without, in this case, a quarterdeck and forecastle.

The *Worcester* of *The Ionion Mission* is a 74-gun ship of two decks – a true ship-of-the-line. The actual name was not used for a 74-gun ship of that period but the class to which she was said to belong, known to sea officers as 'the forty thieves', really did exist. There is, however, some deviation from the real facts. The first ship of the class was completed in 1809 but the fortieth was not launched until 1822; the nickname does not seem to have been used before then. They were despised by the sea officers, perhaps unfairly. Their design and building, though, uninspired was generally competent.[12]

After his transfer out of the *Worcester*, Aubrey returned to the *Surprise*, and that ship is dominant in the remaining books of the series. In his depiction of the ships of the Napoleonic era, Patrick O'Brian shows he has a firm grasp of the complexities of naval architecture as he does of a host of other skills and specialisms, a grasp which enables him to write of that period in a uniquely authoritative and entertaining way.

This essay is taken from
Patrick O'Brian, Critical Appreciations and a Bibliography,
edited by A. E. Cunningham, and is reprinted here by
kind permission of The British Library

ENDNOTES

1   Patrick O'Brian, *The Surgeon's Mate* (London: Collins, 1980), pp. 149 & 153.

2   Patrick O'Brian, *Master and Commander* (London: Collins, 1970), pp. 13, 27, 44, 48 & 53.

3   Patrick O'Brian, *Post Captain* (London: Collins, 1972), pp. 157 & 175.

4   Patrick O'Brian, *H.M.S. Surprise* (London: Collins, 1973), pp. 77–78.

5   Ibid, pp. 123–124; William James, *The Naval History of Great Britain from the Declaration of War by France …* (London: [n.pub.], 1822–24), II, pp. 406–412; Dudley Pope, *The Black Ship* (London: Weidenfeld & Nicolson, 1963).

6   James, *The Naval History*, II, p. 406.

7 William Falconer, *An Universal Dictionary of the Marine*, ed. W. Burney, rev. edn (London: [n. pub.], 1815), p. 14.

8 Brian Lavery, *The Arming and Fitting of the English Ship of War*, (London: Conway Maritime, 1987), p. 299

9 James, *The Naval History*, II, p. 405.

10 Ibid, p. 156.

11 O'Brian, *The Surgeon's Mate*, p. 156.

12 Brian Lavery, *The Shop of the Line* (London: Conway Maritime, 1983), I, 134–139 & 188–189.

ABOUT THE AUTHOR

Patrick O'Brian was born in 1914 and published his first book, *Caesar*, when he was only fifteen. He went on to write stories and poems throughout his life, published acclaimed biographies of Picasso and the naturalist Joseph Banks, and also translated from the French, including Simone de Beauvoir, among others.

In the early 1960s he began work on the idea that, over the next four decades, evolved into the twenty-novel long Aubrey–Maturin series (with an extra unfinished volume published posthumously), covering a period of twenty years during the height of the Napoleonic wars and traversing much of the globe, which firmly established O'Brian as one of the foremost and best-loved storytellers of the twentieth century. He married Mary Tolstoy in 1945, and they spent the rest of their lives together in Collioure in France, she typing out all of his manuscripts through their many drafts, he dedicating all of the books to her.

In 1995 Patrick O'Brian was awarded the CBE, and in 1997 he received an honorary doctorate of letters from Trinity College, Dublin. He died in January 2000 at the age of eighty-five.

The Complete Short Stories

Patrick O'Brian is acclaimed as one of the greatest historical novelists of the twentieth century, celebrated throughout the world for his masterful *roman fleuve*, the Aubrey–Maturin series. But he was also a prolific writer of short stories, and it is in this form that he first made his mark.

Encompassing stories written in his unvarnished youth to tales told by a seasoned traveller, this is the most comprehensive collection of O'Brian's short fiction ever published. It is a treasure chest, overflowing with riches, containing more than sixty tales, including rarities, uncollected works, and forgotten jewels that have been out of print for decades.

These are stories of friendship, travel, adventure and the wonders of the natural world. Some are enchantingly funny, others exciting, terrifying, passionate. All of them prove Patrick O'Brian to be a true master of the form.

With an introduction by Nikolai Tolstoy, the author's stepson, *The Complete Short Stories* is an essential addition to any bookshelf, certain to enchant O'Brian admirers as well as readers who are fortunate enough to be journeying with him for the very first time.

'O'Brian writes like a man to whom writing comes as easily as breathing: precisely, fluently, economically.'
JANE SHILLING, *Sunday Telegraph*

'There are two types of people in the world: Patrick O'Brian fans, and people who haven't read him yet.'
LUCY EYRE, *Guardian*